The Thin Santa Claus

The Chicken Yard That Was a Christmas Stocking

Ellis Parker Butler

Alpha Editions

This edition published in 2023

ISBN : 9789357940337

Design and Setting By
Alpha Editions
www.alphaedis.com
Email - info@alphaedis.com

Contents

THE THIN SANTA CLAUS

Mrs. Gratz opened her eyes and looked out at the drizzle that made the Christmas morning gray. Her bed stood against the window, and it was easy for her to look out; all she had to do was to roll over and pull the shade aside. Having looked at the weather she rolled again on to the broad flat of her back and made herself comfortable for awhile, for there was no reason why she should get up until she felt like it.

"Such a Christmas!" she said good-naturedly to herself. "I guess such weathers is bad for Santy Claus. Mebby it is because of such weathers he don't come by my house. I don't blame him. So muddy!"

She let her eyes close indolently. Not yet was she hungry enough to imagine the tempting odour of fried bacon and eggs, and she idly slipped into sleep again. She was in no hurry. She was never in a hurry. What is the use of being in a hurry when you own a good little house and have money in the bank and are a widow? What is the use of being in a hurry, anyway? Mrs. Gratz was always placid and fat, and she always had been. What is the use of having money in the bank and a good little house if you are not placid and fat? Mrs. Gratz lay on her back and slept, placidly and fatly, with her mouth open, as if she expected Santa Claus to pass by and drop a present into it. Her dreams were pleasant.

It was no disappointment to Mrs. Gratz that Santa Claus had not come to her house. She had not expected him. She did not even believe in him.

"Yes," she had told Mrs. Flannery, next door, as she handed a little parcel of toys over the fence for the little Flannerys, "once I believes in such a Santy Claus myself, yet. I make me purty good times then. But now I'm too old. I don't believe in such things. But I make purty good times, still. I have a good little house, and money in the bank—"

Suddenly Mrs. Gratz closed her mouth and opened her eyes. She smelled imaginary bacon frying. She felt real hunger. She slid out of bed and began to dress herself, and she had just buttoned her red flannel petticoat around her wide waist when she heard a silence, and paused. For a full minute she stood, trying to realize what the silence meant. The English sparrows were chirping as usual and making enough noise, but through their bickerings the silence still annoyed Mrs. Gratz, and then, quite suddenly again, she knew. Her chickens were not making their usual morning racket.

"I bet you I know what it is, sure," she said, and continued to dress as placidly as before. When she went down she found that she had won the bet.

A week before two chickens had been stolen from her coop, and she had had a strong padlock put on the chicken house. Now the padlock was pried open, and the chicken house was empty, and nine hens and a rooster were gone. Mrs. Gratz stooped and entered the low gate and surveyed the vacant chicken yard placidly. If they were gone, they were gone.

"Such a Santy Claus!" she said good-naturedly. "I don't like such a Santy Claus—taking away and not bringing! Purty soon he don't have such a good name any more if he keeps up doing like this. People likes the bringing Santy Claus. I guess they don't think much of the taking-away business. He gets a bad name quick enough if he does this much."

She turned to bend her head to look into the vacant chicken house and stood still. She put out her foot and touched something her eyes had lighted upon, and the thing moved. It was a purse of worn, black leather, soaked by the drizzle, but still holding the bend that comes to men's purses when worn long in a back trouser pocket. One end of the purse was muddy and pressed deep into the soft soil where a heel had tramped on it. Mrs. Gratz bent and picked it up.

There was nine hundred dollars in bills in the purse. Mrs. Gratz stood still while she counted the bills, and as she counted her hands began to tremble, and her knees shook, and she sank on the door-sill of the chicken house and laughed until the tears rolled down her face. Occasionally she stopped to wipe her eyes, and the flood of laughter gradually died away into ripples of intermittent giggles that were like sobs after sorrow. Mrs. Gratz had no great sense of humour, but she could see the fun of finding nine hundred dollars. It was enough to make her laugh, so she laughed.

"Goodness, such a Santy Claus!" she exclaimed with a final sigh of pleasure. "Such a Christmas present from Santy Claus! No wonder he is so fat yet when he eats ten chickens in one night already. But I don't kick. I like me that Santy Claus all right. I believes in him purty good after this, I bet!"

She went at once to tell Mrs. Flannery, and Mrs. Flannery was far more excited about it than Mrs. Gratz had been. She said it was the Hand of Retribution paying back the chicken thief, and the Hand of Justice repaying Mrs. Gratz for sending toys to the little Flannerys, and Pure Luck giving Mrs. Gratz what she always got, and a number of other things.

"'Tis the luck of ye, Mrs. Gratz, ma'am," she said, "and often I do be sayin' it is the Dutch for luck, meanin' no disrespect to ye, and the fatter the luckier, as I often told me old man, rest his soul, and him so thin! And Christmas mornin' at that, ma'am, which is nothin' at all but th' judgment of hivin on th' dirty chicken thief, pickin' such a day for his thievin', when there's plenty other days in th' year for him. Keep th' money, ma'am, for 't is yours by good rights, and I knew there would some good come till ye th' minute ye handed me th' prisints for the kids. The good folks sure all gits ther reward in this world, only some don't, an' I'm only sorry mine is a pig instid of chickens, but not wishin' ye hadn't th' money yersilf, at all, but who would come to steal a pig, and them such loud squealers? And who do you suspicion it was, Mrs. Gratz, ma'am?"

"I think mebby I got me a present from Santy Claus, yes?" said Mrs. Gratz.

"And hear th' woman!" said Mrs. Flannery. "Do ye hear that now? Well, true for ye, ma'am, and stick to it, for there's no tellin' who'll be claimin' th' money, and if ever Santy Claus brought a thing to a mortal soul 't was him brought ye that. And 't was only yesterday ye was sayin' ye had no belief in him!"

"Yesterday I don't have no beliefs in him," said Mrs. Gratz. "To-day I have plenty of beliefs in him. I like him plenty. I don't care if he comes every year."

"Sure not," said Mrs. Flannery, "and you with th' nine hundred dollars in yer pocket. I'd be glad of the chanst. I'd believe in him, mesilf, for four hundred and fifty."

That afternoon Mrs. Flannery, whose excitement had not abated in the least, went over to Mrs. Gratz's to spend the afternoon talking to her about the money. She felt that it was good to be that near it, at any rate, and when one can make a whole afternoon's conversation out of what Mrs. Casey said to Mrs. O'Reilly about Mrs. McNally, it is a shame to miss a chance to talk about nine hundred dollars. Mrs. Flannery was rocking violently and talking rapidly, and Mrs. Gratz was slowly moving her rocker and answering in monosyllables, when some one knocked at the door. Mrs. Gratz answered the knock.

**"He looked like a man who had lost nine hundred
dollars, but he did not look like Santa Claus"**

Her visitor was a tall, thin man, and he had a slouch hat, which
he held in his hands as he talked. He seemed nervous, and his
face wore a worried look—extremely worried. He looked like
a man who had lost nine hundred dollars, but he did not look
like Santa Claus. He was thinner and not so jolly-looking. At
first Mrs. Gratz had no idea that Santa Claus was standing
before her, for he did not have a sleigh-bell about him, and he
had left his red cotton coat with the white batting trimming at
home. He stood in the door playing with his hat, unable to
speak. He seemed to have some delicacy about beginning.

"Well, what it is?" said Mrs. Gratz.

Her visitor pulled himself together with an effort.

"Well, ma'am, I'll tell you," he said frankly. "I'm a chicken buyer. I buy chickens. That's my business—dealin' in poultry—so I came out to-day to buy some chickens—"

"On Christmas Day?" asked Mrs. Gratz.

"Well," said the man, moving uneasily from one foot to the other, "I did come on Christmas Day, didn't I? I don't deny that, ma'am. I did come on Christmas Day. I'd like to go out and have a look at your chickens—"

"It ain't so usual for buyers to come buying chickens on Christmas Day, is it?" interposed Mrs. Gratz, good-naturedly.

"Well, no, it ain't, and that's a fact," said the man uneasily. "But I always do. The people I buy chickens for is just as apt to want to eat chicken one day as another day—and more so. Turkey on Christmas Day, and chicken the next, for a change—that's what they always tell me. So I have to buy chickens every day. I hate to, but I have to, and if I could just go out and look around your chicken yard—"

It was right there that Mrs. Gratz had a suspicion that Santa Claus stood before her.

"But I don't sell such a chicken yard, yet," she said. The man wiped his forehead.

"Sure not," he said nervously. "I was goin' to say look around your chicken yard and see the chickens. I can't buy chickens without I see them, can I? Some folks might, but I can't with the kind of customers I've got. I've got mighty particular customers, and I pay extra prices so as to get the best for them, and when I go out and look around the chicken yard—"

"How much you pay for such nice, big, fat chickens, mebby?" asked Mrs. Gratz.

"Well, I'll tell you," said the man. "Seven cents a pound is regular, ain't it? Well, I pay twelve. I'll give you twelve cents, and pay you right now, and take all the chickens you've got. That's my rule. But, if you want to let me go out and see the chickens first, and pick out the kind my regular customers like, I pay twenty cents a pound. But I won't pay twenty cents without I can see the chickens first."

"Sure," said Mrs. Gratz. "I wouldn't do it, too. Mebby I go out and bring in a couple such chickens for you to look at? Yes?"

"No, don't!" said the man impulsively. "Don't do it! It wouldn't be no good. I've got to see the chickens on the hoof, as I might say."

"On the hoofs?" said Mrs. Gratz. "Such poultry don't have no hoofs."

"Runnin' around," explained the visitor. "Runnin' around in the coop. I can tell if a chicken has got any disease that my trade wouldn't like, if I see it runnin' around in the coop. There's a lot in the way a chicken runs. In the way it h'ists up its leg, for instance. That's what the trade calls 'on the hoof.' So I'll just go out and have a look around the coop—"

"For twenty cents a pound anybody could let buyers see their chickens on the hoof, I guess," said Mrs. Gratz.

"Now, that's the way to talk!" exclaimed the man.

"Only but I ain't got any such chickens," said Mrs. Gratz. "So it ain't of use to look how they walk. So good-bye."

"Now, say—" said the man, but Mrs. Gratz closed the door in his face.

"I guess such a Santy Claus came back yet," said Mrs. Gratz when she went into the room where Mrs. Flannery was sitting. "But it ain't any use. He don't leave many more such presents."

"Th' impidince of him!" exclaimed Mrs. Flannery.

"For nine hundred dollars I could be impudent, too," said Mrs. Gratz calmly. "But I don't like such nowadays Santy Clauses, coming back all the time. Once, when I believes in Santy Clauses, they don't come back so much."

The thin Santa Claus had not gone far. He had crossed the street and stood gazing at Mrs. Gratz's door, and now he crossed again and knocked. Mrs. Gratz arose and went to the door.

"I believe he comes back once yet," she said to Mrs. Flannery, and opened the door. He had, indeed, come back.

"Now see here," he said briskly, "ain't your name Mrs. Gratz? Well, I knowed it was, and I knowed you was a widow lady, and that's why I said I was a chicken buyer. I didn't want to frighten you. But I ain't no chicken buyer."

"No?" asked Mrs. Gratz.

"No, I ain't. I just said that so I could get a look at your chicken yard. I've got to see it. What I am is chicken-house inspector for the Ninth Ward, and the Mayor sent me up here to inspect your chicken house, and I've got to do it before I go away, or lose my job. I'll go right out now, and it'll be all over in a minute—"

"I guess it ain't some use," said Mrs. Gratz. "I guess I don't keep any more chickens. They go too easy. Yesterday I have plenty, and to-day I haven't any."

"That's it!" said the thin Santa Claus. "That's just it! That's the way toober-chlosis bugs act—quick like that. They're a bad epidemic—toober-chlosis bugs is. You see how they act— yesterday you have chickens, and last night the toober-chlosis bugs gets at them, and this morning they've eat them all up."

"Goodness!" exclaimed Mrs. Gratz without emotion. "With the fedders and the bones, too?"

"Sure," said the thin Santa Claus. "Why, them toober-chlosis bugs is perfectly ravenous. Once they git started they eat feathers and bones and feet and all—a chicken hasn't no chance at all. That's why the Mayor sent me up here. He heard all your chickens was gone, and gone quick, and he says to me, 'Toober-chlosis bugs!' That's what he says, and he says, 'You ain't doing your duty. You ain't inspected Mrs. Gratz's chicken coop. You go and do it, or you're fired, see?' He says that, and he says, 'You inspect Mrs. Gratz's coop, and you kill off them bugs before they git into her house and eat her all up—bones and all.'"

"And fedders?" asked Mrs. Gratz calmly.

"No, he didn't say feathers. This ain't nothing to fool about. It's serious. So I'll go right out and have a look—"

"I guess such bugs ain't been in *my* coop last night," said Mrs. Gratz carelessly. "I aint afraid of such bugs in winter time."

"Well, that's where you make your mistake," said the thin Santa Claus. "Winter is just the bad time for them bugs. The more a toober-chlosis bug freezes up the more dangerous it is. In summer they ain't so bad—they're soft like and squash up when a chicken gits them, but in winter they freeze up hard and git brittle. Then a chicken comes along and grabs one, and it busts into a thousand pieces, and each piece turns into a new toober-chlosis bug and busts into a thousand pieces, and so on, and the chicken gits all filled full of toober-chlosis bugs before it knows it. When a chicken snaps up one toober-chlosis bug it has a million in it inside of half an hour and that chicken don't last long, and when the bugs make for the house—What's that on your dress there now?"

Mrs. Gratz looked at her arm indifferently.

"Nothing," she said.

"I thought mebby it was a toober-chlosis bug had got on you already," said the thin Santa Claus. "If it was you would be all eat up inside of half an hour. Them bugs is awful rapacious."

"Yes?" inquired Mrs. Gratz with interest. "Such strong bugs, too, is it not?"

"You bet they are strong—" began the stranger.

"I should think so," interrupted Mrs. Gratz, "to smash up padlocks on such chicken houses. You make me afraid of such bugs. I don't dare let you go out there to get your bones and feet all eat up by them. I guess not!"

"Well, you see—you see—" said the thin Santa Claus, puzzled, and then he cheered up. "You see, I ain't afraid of them. I've been fumigated against them. Fumigated and antiskep— antiskepticized. I've been vaccinated against them by the Board of Health. I'll show you the mark on my arm, if you want to see it."

"No, don't," said Mrs. Gratz. "I let you go and look in that chicken coop if you want to, but it ain't no use. There ain't nothing there."

The thin Santa Claus paused and looked at Mrs. Gratz with suspicion.

"Why? Did you find it?" he asked.

"Find what?" asked Mrs. Gratz innocently, and the thin Santa Claus sighed and walked around to the back of the house. Mrs. Gratz went with him.

As Mrs. Gratz watched the thin man search the chicken yard for toober-chlosis bugs all doubt that he was her Santa Claus left her mind. He made a most minute investigation, but he did it more as a man might search for a lost purse than as a health officer would search for germs. He even got down on his hands and knees and poked under the chicken house with a stick, and, when he had combed the chicken yard thoroughly and had looked all through the chicken house, he even searched the denuded vegetable garden in the back yard, and looked over the fence into Mrs. Flannery's yard. Evidently he was not pleased with his investigation, for he did not even say good-bye to Mrs. Gratz, but went away looking mad and cross.

When Mrs. Gratz went into her house she took her seat in her rocking-chair and began rocking herself calmly and slowly.

"'T was him done it, sure," said Mrs. Flannery.

"I don't like such come-agains, much," said Mrs. Gratz placidly. "I try me to believe in such a Santy Claus, but I like not such come-agains. In Germany did not Santy Claus come back so much. I don't like a Santy Claus should be so anxious. Still I believes in him, but, if he has too many such come-agains, I don't believe in him much."

"I would be settin' th' police on him, Santy Claus or no Santy Claus," said Mrs. Flannery vindictively; "th' mean chicken thief!"

"Oh," said Mrs. Gratz easily, "I guess I don't care much should a nine-hundred-dollar Santy Claus steal some chickens. I ain't mad."

But she was a little provoked when another knock came at the door a few minutes later, and when, on opening it, she saw the thin Santa Claus before her again.

"So!" she said, "Santy Claus is back yet once!"

"What's that?" asked the man suspiciously.

"I say, what it is you want?" said Mrs. Gratz.

"Oh!" said the man. "Well, I ain't a-goin' to fool with you no longer, Mrs. Gratz. I'm a-goin' to tell you right out what I am and who I am. I'm a detective of the police, and I'm looking up a mighty bad character."

"I guess I know right where you find one," said Mrs. Gratz politely.

"Now, don't be funny," said the thin Santa Claus peevishly. "Mebby you noticed I didn't say nothing when you spoke about that padlock being busted? Mebby you noticed how careful I looked over your chicken coop, and how I looked over the fence into the next yard? Well, I won't fool you. I ain't no chicken-yard inspector, and I ain't no chicken buyer—them was just my detective disguises. I'm out detecting a chicken thief—just a plain, ordinary chicken thief—and what I come for is clues."

"Yes?" said Mrs. Gratz. "And what is it, such cloos? I haven't any clooses."

The thin Santa Claus seemed provoked.

"Now, look here!" he said. "You may think this is funny, but it isn't. I have got to catch that chicken thief or I'll lose my job, and I can't catch him unless I have some clues to catch him with. Now, didn't you have some chickens stolen last night?"

"Chickens?" asked Mrs. Gratz. "No, I didn't have chickens stolen. Such toober-chlosis bugs eat them. With fedders, too. And bones. Right off the hoofs, ain't it a pity?"

It may have been a blush of shame, but it was more like a flush of anger, that overspread the face of the thin Santa Claus. He stared hard at the placid German face of Mrs. Gratz, and decided she was too stupid to mean it—that she was not teasing him.

"You don't catch on," he said. "You see, there ain't any such things as toober-chlosis bugs. I just made that up as a sort of detective disguise. Them chickens wasn't eat by no bugs at all—they was stole. See? A chicken thief come right into the coop and stole them. Do you think any kind of a bug could pry off a padlock?"

Mrs. Gratz seemed to let this sink into her mind and to revolve there, and get to feeling at home, before she answered.

"No," she said at length, "I guess not. But Santy Claus could do it. Such a big, fat man. Sure he could do it."

"Why, you—" began the thin man crossly, and then changed his tone. "There ain't no such thing as Santy Claus," he said as one might speak to a child—but even a chicken thief would not tell a child such a thing, I hope.

"No?" queried Mrs. Gratz sadly. "No Santy Claus? And I was scared of it, myself, with such toober-chlosis bugs around. He should not to have gone into such a chicken coop with so many bugs busting up all over. He had a right to have fumigated himself, once. And now he ain't. He's all eat up, on the hoof, bones, and feet and all. And such a kind man, too."

The thin Santa Claus frowned. He had half an idea that Mrs. Gratz was fooling with him, and when he spoke it was crisply.

"Now, see here," he said, "last night somebody broke into your chicken coop and stole all your chickens. I know that. And he's been stealing chickens all around this town, and all around this part of the country, too, and I know that. And this stealing has got to stop. I've got to catch that thief. And to catch him I've got to have a clue. A clue is something he has left around, or dropped, where he was stealing. Now, did that chicken thief drop any clues in your chicken yard? That's what I want to know—did he drop any clues?"

"Mebby, if he dropped some cloos, those toober-chlosis bugs eat them up," suggested Mrs. Gratz. "They eats bones and fedders; mebby they eats cloos, too."

"Now, ain't that smart?" sneered the thin Santa Claus. "Don't you think you're funny? But I'll tell you the clue I'm looking for. Did that thief drop a pocketbook, or anything like that?"

"Oh, a pocketbook!" said Mrs. Gratz. "How much should be in such a pocketbook, mebby?"

"Nine hundred dollars," said the thin Santa Claus promptly.

"Goodness!" exclaimed Mrs. Gratz. "So much money all in one cloos! Come out to the chicken yard once; I'll help hunt for cloos, too."

The thin Santa Claus stood a minute looking doubtfully at Mrs. Gratz. Her face was large and placid and unemotional.

"Well," he said with a sigh, "it ain't much use, but I'll try it again."

When he had gone, after another close search of the chicken yard and coop, Mrs. Gratz returned to her friend, Mrs. Flannery.

"Purty soon I don't belief any more in Santy Claus at all," she said. "Purty soon I have more beliefs in chicken thiefs than in Santy Claus. Yet a while I beliefs in him, but, one more of those come-agains, and I don't."

"He'll not be comin' back any more," said Mrs. Flannery positively. "I'm wonderin' he came at all, and the jail so handy. All ye have t' do is t' call a cop."

"Sure!" said Mrs. Gratz. "But it is not nice I should put Santy Claus in jail. Such a liberal Santy Claus, too."

"Have it yer own way, ma'am," said Mrs. Flannery. "I'll own 'tis some different whin chickens is stole. 'Tis hard to expind th' affections on a bunch of chickens, but, if any one was t' steal my pig, t' jail he would go, Santy Claus or no Santy Claus. Not but what ye have a kind heart anyway, ma'am, not wantin' t' put th' poor fellow in jail whin he has already lost nine hundred dollars, which, goodness knows, ye might have t' hand back, was th' law t' take a hand in it."

"So!" said Mrs. Gratz. "Such is the law, yet? All right, I don't belief in chicken thiefs, no matter how much he comes again. I stick me to Santy Claus. Always will I belief in Santy Claus. Chicken thiefs gives, and wants to take away again, but Santy Claus is always giving and never taking."

"Ye 're fergettin' th' chickens that was took," suggested Mrs. Flannery.

"Took?" said Mrs. Gratz.

"Tooken," Mrs. Flannery corrected.

"Tooked?" said Mrs. Gratz. "I beliefs me not in Santy Claus that way. I beliefs he is a good old man. For givings I beliefs in Santy Claus, but for takings I beliefs in toober-chlosis bugs."

"An' th' busted padlock, then?" asked Mrs. Flannery.

"Ach!" exclaimed Mrs. Gratz. "Them reindeers is so frisky, yet. They have a right to kick up and bust it, mebby."

Mrs. Flannery sighed.

"'T is a grand thing t' have faith, ma'am," she said.

"Y-e-s," said Mrs. Gratz indolently, "that's nice. And it is nice to have nine hundred dollars more in the bank, ain't it?"

THE END

www.ingramcontent.com/pod-product-compliance
Lightning Source LLC
Chambersburg PA
CBHW022343280326
41934CB00006B/767